LISA RYAN CAMPBELL

Explicit

THE *ex* FILES

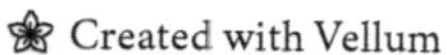 Created with Vellum

For my Readers.

CHAPTER ONE

Colleen

I could see the red and blue flashing lights when I was about a quarter of a mile from my home. They commanded the attention of the street traffic forcing anyone who passed by to slow down and take a look to see what had happened. At first, I thought it was a car accident—maybe a driver enjoying their weekend too much despite the fact that it was a cold and rainy February night. But as I pulled onto my street, I saw that the flashing lights of the police and emergency vehicles were in front of my house. No, not exactly my house, but my neighbor's house. Yellow caution tape ran along the perimeter of Will's home, and I instantly felt the hair rising on the back of my neck.

I had to park across the street, since the emergency vehicles were blocking my driveway. I quickly grabbed my purse and umbrella and as soon as I stepped out of my car, I felt the eyes of many of my neighbors who all looked to be huddled together with their umbrellas raised and darting looks between me and Will's house.

"What happened?" I joined the crowd of onlookers and asked no one in particular.

One woman, balancing an umbrella and an antsy toddler in her arms, spoke up immediately, as though she were waiting for me to ask and eager to relay the news.

"Somebody broke into Will's house and killed him!"

I already suspected something terrible had happened, but before I could digest the news, another man interjected himself in the conversation.

"It wasn't a break-in. Apparently, he opened the door to this person and was shot. That's what the police are saying. I was out walking my dog. I passed by his house, saw that the door was open and a pair of legs were sticking out the door."

I stepped closer to the man, hanging onto every word of his recount. He looked shaken from the night's events.

"Booters, my dog, started barking and whining, so I knew something was wrong. I called out to him, but he didn't answer. So, I walked up to the steps and when I came to the body, I saw his face…"

He paused, and I guessed he was trying to calm his nerves at recalling what must have been a gruesome sight. "His face was completely gone. I backed up, took Booters home and called 911."

He angled his head toward the swarm of police vehicles. "They interviewed me as soon as they got here. They interviewed all of us."

"They asked me if I knew of any enemies he might've had," another woman said. "But I barely knew him. I did always think it was odd that he chose to live in Marina, when a man with his wealth could afford a place in Nob Hill or even Cliffside."

"Maybe it was a scorned woman," someone else

suggested. "He did like to have parties and bring women home."

My back involuntarily stiffened at that last remark. Figuring I'd gotten as much information as I was going to get, I politely excused myself from my neighbors and walked slowly across the street toward my house. All the while, I kept my eyes trained on Will's home, trying to make sense of what I was feeling. Was it sadness, anger, confusion? Ultimately, I decided that right now, I felt nothing. I was numb. Maybe delayed shock. Will was my next-door neighbor, and even though our interactions had been reduced to a simple wave or hesitant "Good morning", he had been alive. He had been a living human being, and now he was gone. But why? Who would want to kill him?

I made my way up the steps leading to my front door, let myself inside, and closed the door behind me. But just as I stepped a few inches into the living area, a brusque knock sounded, causing me to jump in surprise. I took a few deep breaths to calm my nerves then turned back around, switched on the foyer light and opened the door to a slender black woman dressed in jeans, boots and a black bomber jacket and holding up a badge.

"Good evening, ma'am. I'm Sergeant Lena Daniels with the San Francisco police."

I nodded. "Good evening, Sergeant. I'm Colleen."

"I'm sorry to bother you, but I'm sure you're aware that your next-door neighbor, Will Evans, was killed tonight."

I breathed in and out again. "The neighbors told me he was shot by an intruder."

"Yes, that's right," she replied. "We're canvassing the neighborhood to see if anyone saw or heard anything that might shed some light on what happened. We came by earlier to speak with you, but you weren't home. Just now, one of my officers saw you come in the house and notified me."

"I only just arrived. I was working late tonight."

In actuality, I'd left work hours ago, but had been driving around the city all this time, feeling as though I were stuck in a void. I should tell her that, but for now, I just stayed with the lie.

Sergeant Daniels put her badge away and angled her head slightly to one side. "Do you mind if I come inside for a minute to speak with you?"

"No, of course not." I stepped to the side, allowing her to enter.

As I closed the door behind her, I wondered if I just made a big mistake by letting her in my home to interview me. Maybe she was astute enough to easily recognize the first lie I told and wanted to see how many more lies I would tell her. That suspicion heightened when I turned around to find her watching me with a keen eye. She was an attractive woman with a complexion slightly darker than my own. We shared the same color brown eyes, but hers were bold, fierce and silently daring me to try to deceive her.

"Can I offer you coffee, Sergeant," I asked, gesturing for her to take a seat in the living room.

"No, I won't take up too much of your time," she said, taking off her jacket, sitting down and pulling out a notepad. "Let's start with your full name."

"Colleen Strayer."

"Do you live alone, Ms. Strayer?"

"Yes."

"I know you said were at work most of the day, but do you recall seeing anything out of the ordinary today or in the past few days next door or even around the neighborhood?"

I made an effort to look as if I was actually thinking about the question, so she wouldn't think I was deliberately rushing this interview along. After a short but appropriate amount of time passed, I shook my head and frowned in regret.

"No, nothing."

"No strange sightings or activity next door?"

Does the sight of him having sex with a woman while watching me count as strange activity?

I shook my head again. "No. Will kept to himself a lot. Most of us do in this neighborhood. I think tonight was the first time I actually spoke to my neighbors in the six months I've lived here."

Sergeant Daniels smile politely and looked around. "It's a nice area, and you have a beautiful home. I've always wanted to live in a place like this, but the rent always seemed a bit out of reach. Then again, I do only make a cop's salary."

I wanted to tell her that after tonight, I may not be able to afford to live in this beautiful place, but that would only lead to more questions, and I wanted to get this over with as quickly as possible.

"May I ask what you do for a living, Ms. Strayer?"

I didn't mean to hesitate, but I did, and I could tell she picked up on it when her eyes slightly narrowed.

"I'm the Chief Financial Officer for Lomax Industries."

When her eyes narrowed even further and a frown began to form on her brow, I knew she'd done her homework on Will long before she came to the scene of his murder.

"From my understanding, Will Evans was the primary shareholder and CEO of Lomax Industries."

"That's right," I confirmed.

"The company belonged to his mother's family and was passed down to Will after her death."

I nodded again. *Here it comes.*

"You're telling me your next-door neighbor was also your boss?"

CHAPTER TWO

Will

$\mathcal{I}$ wonder if there was ever a study done on the reaction of humans to seeing a dead body for the first time. Yes, it would be pretty shitty to take a horde of people and bring them into a room one by one where each unsuspecting person would be confronted with a bloody corpse while scientists stood by, disconnected, taking notes and analyzing results.

But with all that said, I'm sure the findings would be both interesting and varied. Many would scream, some would back away in fear, while others would get angry, demanding to know what the fuck was going on. But a few, a select few, would probably just stare at the body waiting for delayed shock to set in, and knowing it wasn't going to come. This was my reaction at seeing my friend's body, wearing my clothes and sprawled out at my front door with his face blown half off.

I looked at him, covered my mouth with one hand and

took several deep breaths. It struck me that I knew exactly what must have happened, the colossal mistake, and what really should have happened. Then, my next thought came almost immediately—I had to get out of here. Even with the heavy downpour and thunder, someone would have heard the shot and called the police. In fact, I was surprised the police weren't already here. Had I just missed the murderer? That thought convinced me to move faster.

I stepped around Troy's body and raced upstairs careful not to turn on any more lights and shutting off any lights that were already on. This was my house, after all, and I knew its layout well enough to get what I needed in the dark.

My first stop was the bedroom, specifically the walk-in closet where I felt along one of the many top shelves until my fingers touched the straps of a backpack. I pulled it down and began stuffing it with underwear, socks, a few t-shirts and a couple pairs of pants. I then changed clothes quickly out of my shirt and dress slacks into a dark-colored t-shirt and a pair of jeans. I then made my way to the wall safe. As I turned the dial to the combination lock, I heard the distant wail of police sirens. Panic began to steadily rise up my spine, but I kept focused and opened the safe. Into the backpack went a few stacks of rubber-banded money, my passport just in case, and a gun.

I slammed the safe door closed, put on a jacket and baseball cap and stepped out of the closet. As the sirens grew louder, I knew without a doubt they were coming to this address. I tried to think of anything else I needed, and then another thought assaulted me. If what I suspected was true, then no one could know that it was Troy's body lying in the foyer—at least for now. When the police got here, I was going to be presumed dead, and I needed to stay that way. Slinging the backpack over one shoulder, I felt my way through the dark to my nightstand by the bed. I opened the top drawer, pulled out a flashlight, switched it on and whipped it around the room. The bed was made. Not just made, but it looked exactly the same way I left it when I went out of town. Troy hadn't slept in here. Thinking fast, I rumpled up the covers and sheets and put my wallet and house keys on the nightstand. Then I ran to the guest bedroom, with the flashlight leading my way. The room was clean and tidy and the bed was made. Helen, my housekeeper who came in the mornings, must have seen to that. I found Troy's overnight bag in the corner and grabbed it. He was only staying for the weekend and was never one to unpack. He liked living out of his suitcase, and right now, I was grateful for that.

The sirens were now blasting through the sounds of the storm as police cars turned onto the street. I raced down the stairs, knowing I had only seconds left and that it was too late to go out the front door. I ran to the kitchen, and by sheer luck, spotted Troy's wallet and keys on the kitchen counter. I grabbed them on the run, yanked open the door that led to the back patio and let myself out just as the deafening shouts of police came from the front door. I hurried down the back steps and nearly slipped from the slick wet rain pelting down on every surface. I quickly regained my balance and looked around.

Where? Where do I go?

As soon as the police saw Troy's body, this house will be surrounded. I couldn't stay back here. Then I stared at the wall that separated my house from my neighbor to the right.

Colleen.

I didn't know if she was home, but whether she was or not, I was going over that wall. I flung Troy's duffel over first and made a running jump to launch myself high enough to reach the ledge. My height was enough to get me there, but the rain and the rubber soles of my sneakers were making it tough to climb over the wall. Still, the fact that police were storming my house at this very minute, and I was only seconds away from one of them looking out the window or coming into the backyard to catch me vaulting over into my neighbor's property, was all the motivation I needed to heave myself up and over the wall.

I fell to the ground and stayed there for a long time, willing my adrenaline to slow down and my breathing to return to normal. There was a swarm of activity in my house now with police and EMTs everywhere. I peered up at Colleen's house, and saw it was dark inside. I looked down at my watch, read the time and assumed it was too early for her to be in bed. Knowing the company's CFO, she'd still be at the office. I looked toward the steps that led up to her back patio. These homes were all built pretty similar, and just like mine, her steps had an alcove at the bottom that was just large enough for me to crawl into out of the rain. I did just that, huddled my body as close as possible against the rain and wind chill and waited for her to come home.

She might not let me in, she might not help me at all, given our tension-filled relationship, but I was hoping she would put all that to the side. I had no other choice—I needed her. And that pissed me off.

CHAPTER THREE

Colleen

I sat at my desk with my laptop open with the glare of the screen the only light in the room. After Sergeant Daniels left, I showered, changed into some sweats and immediately logged onto the Lomax Industries website. Just as expected, there was a statement on the company homepage about the "sudden" and "tragic" death of the owner and major shareholder, Will Evans. The public relations department must have been called in as soon as Will's next of kin was notified, who had most likely been his uncle and Chief Operating Officer of the company, Jay Lansing.

Will was dead.

Will was dead, and I should be doing something, practically anything else besides sitting here in my slippers, reading his biography and trying to pinpoint the emotions I was feeling right now.

Will was dead.

Then I finally came to the conclusion that this feeling

welling up inside and choking me was remorse. I was feeling remorse because a man I'd spent one night with was no longer here. A man I once saw as the head of a multimillion-dollar company and a spoiled socialite who only put in face-time during mandatory board meetings to ensure his trust fund was continuing to be replenished. That was unfair, and I don't know when my feelings for him began to change, because before our night together, before I officially met him, I was attracted to him—the tall, dark and lean man with penetrating blue eyes.

I stood and crossed over to the bay window and looked to the left where Will's house was. If the curtains were open, I would have been able to see inside. But now, they were drawn tightly closed, and the house looked so dark and fore-boding—a completely opposite mood from the night I kept envisioning whenever I stood at these windows. That night, his living room was dimly lit by one single lamp. But I could still see clearly how warm and inviting it was. I could still feel how my body turned hot from the two figures writhing in passion. I could still hear my breath catch when he looked at me.

I turned away from the window, shutting down any more memories and went back to my desk where I pulled a notepad and pen from one of the drawers to take notes. I would have to make decisions about the next steps I was going to take in regards to my career and living situation. It was a bold move to apply for the CFO position at Lomax Industries, but I knew with my Doctorate degree in Finance and the fifteen years of experience I had in the field, I was more than qualified for the job. Jay Lansing apparently thought so too when after my third interview, he asked: "When can you start?"

I closed my eyes, vividly reliving the memory of the first time I saw Will and allowed him to buy me a drink, allowed him to lead me to the dance floor and allowed him to take me to his hotel suite.

* * *

It was the weekend I moved from San Diego. A couple of friends of mine helped me pack up my condo and drove up to San Francisco with me to help me get settled into my new home and new city. That night, we all got dressed up and headed out to the club for a girl's night and to celebrate my new job.

The moment I saw him, I knew who he was, since I'd researched his company, including him, thoroughly. That was where I went wrong. I could have turned away. I could have ignored him, but he saw me too, and truth be told, I didn't want to turn back.

"I'm Will Evans," he said, his tailored baby blue dress shirt and black slacks matching his carefree, easy smile.

"Colleen Strayer," I said, then reached out my hand to shake his, all the while holding my breath.

"It's good to meet you, Colleen. Can I buy you and your friends a drink?"

I searched his eyes for any hint of recognition of my name, but either he had the ultimate poker face, or he sincerely didn't know that I was just hired as his company's new CFO. I decided on the latter, and that both disappointed me and eased my mind. I turned around to find that my girl-friends had abandoned me for the dance floor and companions of their own.

"Looks like it's just one drink for me."

He took my hand and gestured for me to take a seat on one of the barstools. "Good, I wasn't sure if I could afford drinks for three women anyway."

I started to laugh, but quickly stopped myself. During my

interview, I was given a glimpse of the company's financial records, and there was no denying the man was loaded. However, I was supposed to be playing the role of a stranger and wasn't supposed to know anything about his wealth.

The night began with drinks and small talk as Will and I exchanged information about ourselves, and I didn't let on that most of what he revealed to me was information I already knew about him. When he finally told me he was the CEO of Lomax Industries, I did my best to feign surprise.

"What do you do for a living," he asked.

"I work in Finance." I looked for any reaction, anything that would reveal he knew more about me than he led on, but he only nodded.

"I'm sorry to say I don't know if my company's finance department is in need of any help. Otherwise, I'd offer you a job," he said, smiling.

I frowned, feeling even more disappointed. I didn't like that he was turning out to be a man not interested in his inheritance. From my research, his company did very well and provided a lot for the community by organizing food drives, providing back to school supplies for kids and donating a healthy chunk of money to soup kitchens, homeless shelters and domestic violence shelters. The generous philanthropy was the main reason I applied for the job, and it was too bad Will wasn't involved in any of it.

"There's nothing you find interesting about your company," I asked.

He shook his head. "I don't typically get involved with any of the day to day business. It's not as if they need me anyway."

"You're the head of the company," I said. "Of course, they need you."

"You think so?"

He raised his glass to his lips and then paused. A far-off

look came into his eyes, and I couldn't decipher it. My first thought was sadness, but somehow, that didn't seem right.

"Every time I walk into that building, I feel like I'm in the way," he continued. "I feel useless, so I find it's easier to just stay away."

Then the look was gone, and those fierce amber eyes were on me. "This is going to sound cliché, but I mean this with all due respect. I like you, Colleen, and unless I'm completely off my game, I'm assuming you like me, too. I'd like to have a dance with you, and then afterwards, I want to leave with you. Is that all right?"

A loud voice inside of me told me to refuse. Will wasn't the type of man I dated. For one thing, I've never been with a wealthy man before; second, I was sure we didn't have anything in common, and third—he was my boss. But a small, quieter voice urged me to just enjoy myself for now and worry about the consequences later. That small voice was very persuasive.

"Yes," I said.

We talked some more in his hotel suite, and I came to realize I'd been wrong about him. Not only was the sex an unbelievable pleasure that I could not get out of my mind, but we had enough in common that would've convinced me to agree to a second date. But then came the morning sunlight that blinded me along with the truth and consequences of my actions. I left the hotel suite early and as quietly as possible while he slept. I never regretted being with him. I only regretted not being completely honest with him.

* * *

I must have fallen asleep at my desk from both exhaustion and sadness, because the next thing I remember was being awoken by a persistent knocking coming from the back door just off the kitchen.

I rose from the desk and checked the time on my cell phone. Who was that at this hour? The knocking grew more insistent and louder to be heard over the rain and thunder. I approached the kitchen warily and decided not to turn on the light. My back door was glass, but there was a sheer curtain that gave some semblance of privacy. I didn't know whether they could see me or not, but I wanted to get a good look at who it was.

I entered the kitchen and crept along the far wall, hoping I wasn't visible in the darkness. Then the knocking came again, startling me at how loud it sounded. Just as I got the idea to pretend I wasn't home, whoever it was peeked through the glass pane and looked right at me.

Shit!

I froze, knowing it was too late to duck back into a dark corner or something. It was a tall dark figure dressed in a jacket and baseball cap, but beyond that, I had no idea who wanted inside my home. Then, whoever it was called my name and when I recognized the voice, I couldn't help but back away in fear. It couldn't be who I thought it was, because that voice belonged to a dead man.

CHAPTER FOUR

Will

If I could somehow telepath to her how important it was for her to just open the door and let me in, I would. Instead, I was left with the choice to knock harder and wave her toward the door. That only made her back away further into the darkened corner of her kitchen. I knew she was just two seconds away from calling the cops, and that was the last thing I wanted.

Earlier, I took a chance, crawled from out of the alcove, crept slowly up to her back porch and saw a glow from her living room. When Colleen passed by, I raised my hand to knock and then quickly put my fist down and moved away from the sliding doors. Someone was in there with her, and I was certain it was the police. I retreated back down the steps, tucked myself back into the small enclosed space and waited some more. After another hour, I looked again. The lamp from her living room was turned off, and I didn't see any movement. After a few knocks, I saw her as soon as she came into the kitchen, looking frightened.

Despite the rain beating down heavily on me, I managed to keep my voice calm and just loud enough to be heard over the rain and through the glass door.

"Colleen, it's me, Will. I'm not going to hurt you."

At the sound of my voice, I could see her grip on the cabinet slightly loosen. I kept talking, hoping to ease more of her tension.

"I'll explain everything. Just please, let me in."

At last, she moved away from the corner, and when she stepped into view, I saw she was dressed for bed with no makeup and her hair swept up into a ponytail. It was such a drastic change from the woman in business suits with a tight bun at the nape of her neck and a serious expression, that I nearly stepped back myself, thinking I had the wrong woman.

Then she opened the door, and I immediately recognized the low, sultry tone of voice that always turned me on.

"Come inside," she said, holding the door open.

I slid inside and promptly dropped my backpack by the door just in case she did a 180 on me and I had to make a quick exit. When I saw she was headed for the light switch, I stopped her.

"No, don't! Leave it off for now."

She dropped her hand to her side instantly, frowned at me and then she said the obvious.

"You're supposed to be dead."

Something told me I should take my time with her when trying to explain this entire fucked up situation. I moved further into the kitchen, took off my ball cap and placed it on the island counter.

"I know. It's all been a terrible misunderstanding."

"The police were all over this neighborhood a half hour ago. Who's the man that's dead in your house?"

"An old college friend."

"The cop working on your case is Sergeant Lena Daniels. I have her card. You need to call her and tell her all of this."

"I can't do that."

"Why? Did you kill him?"

"What? No! You think I'm a killer?" I moved away from the kitchen island and toward her. She backed away only slightly, and I immediately stopped and raised my hands.

"I said I wasn't going to hurt you. I'm not a murderer."

She hesitated and then sighed. "If I really thought that, I wouldn't have let you in. I'm sorry. It's been a long night."

"Something tells me your night hasn't been nearly as long as mine."

Now she looked sheepish. "Take off that wet jacket and come into the living room. I need to show you something."

I shrugged off my jacket and draped it over one of the kitchen table chairs. I then followed her into the living room, where she handed me a towel and gestured to her open laptop on the desk.

"The company homepage is already announcing your death," she said. "Right now, I'm sure your uncle is organizing a midnight meeting to discuss what happens going forward."

"I'm counting on that," I said. "I'm surprised you were here. Being my CFO, you should be in that meeting."

A strange look passed over her face, but before I could question it, it was gone.

"I haven't received any calls yet."

"You will," I said, rubbing the towel over my wet hair, face and neck. "And when you do, I want you to go and record the meeting. I also need—"

"Hold on. Slow down." She raised her hands to halt any further demands from me. "I've just been told by the police and my neighbors that you'd been murdered. And then you show up at my back door in the rain telling me that you don't want to tell the police you're alive and that you need me to record a staff meeting discussing your death?"

"Yes."

She gaped at me.

"I think you should start from the beginning and tell me how your friend got killed and why in the world someone would want to kill you in the first place."

I looked at my wristwatch. I didn't have time for this, but she hadn't yet received the call to come into the office, and in all fairness, I did owe her an explanation since I was here asking for her help. But dammit, couldn't she give that self-righteous act a rest for just one minute? Her hands planted firmly on her full hips and her head raised slightly and eyes narrowed, she was no longer the frightened woman huddled in the dark kitchen. She had assumed her natural role as the woman who I found both aggravating and enticing.

So, I took a moment and told her about coming home and finding Troy dead with a shotgun wound to his face. He'd been wearing my clothes and without the foyer light turned on, he would have been shrouded in darkness to whoever was at the front door. I had to pause at the retelling of Troy's death, because guilt still plagued me.

"I offered him my place to stay for a weekend because he'd been down on his luck. He lost his job, and he and his wife were separated. I was out of town for the weekend and told him to make himself at home."

"I'd just got back into town this evening. When the driver took me home, I immediately knew something wasn't right. My front door was open, and I told him to keep driving. I had him drop me off at the corner, and I took the back alley to my house. There was no sign of a break in from the back door, so I let myself inside, called out his name, and then saw him."

I sat down in one of her arm chairs, reliving the bloody scene at my house.

"Whoever shot Troy mistook him for me. I never would have left...I never would have even offered if I'd known I was putting his life in danger."

Colleen turned her desk chair around and sat down to face me.

"But why," she asked. "Why in the world would someone try to kill you?"

I felt my anger rising. "Not someone. My uncle."

Silence floated between us as I narrowed my gaze at her, waiting to see her reaction. In a span of a few minutes, she seemed to war with so many emotions before settling somewhere between disbelief and anger.

"You're kidding. Jay Lansing wants you, his own nephew, dead? Why?"

"I don't know. Maybe because CEO sounds better than COO."

I was being flippant because my patience was waning. Every second that ticked by was a second closer to my uncle making his move. But if I wanted her help, I was going to have to level with her.

I sighed long and heavy. "It's because I found something. Something that was not meant for me to see. I saw plans of a merger with Southwood Corporation and of a hostile takeover."

"A hostile takeover? You mean…"

"He was trying to take the company away from me. I never would've agreed to a merger. I always wanted Lomax to stay a family-owned business. So did my mother and grandfather. I think Jay always resented the company going to my mother. He wanted to run the business his way, and for a while, I let him. Like I told you the night we met, I didn't have the experience or knowledge to run a multimillion-dollar company, so I left everything up to him. Apparently, he's gotten used to that power and doesn't want to let it go."

"I confronted him about his plans for a merger and pushing me out of my own company and told him I would be conducting a meeting with the Board to vote him out. He didn't know I was leaving for the weekend. I thought I was doing him a courtesy, letting him know ahead of time and giving him the chance to resign with a nice severance package." I paused, clenching my fists. "I simply sign my own death certificate—Troy's death certificate."

"I knew about the merger with Southwood," Colleen said. "We all did. There were the usual rumblings about whether it would affect everyone's jobs, but for the most part, we were all waiting. Jay had my team and I look at the numbers, and from the beginning, they seemed inflated. I suspected the company was hiding money. Their profits were not easily explained, and I came to the conclusion there may be illegal dealings unaware to us. I told Jay this and recommended he cancel the merger. He thanked me for my opinion."

"Then what," I asked.

"Then nothing. A week later, we had a meeting where Jay announced the merger was moving forward. I was surprised, but he seemed very sure about the deal. I wanted..."

"What," I asked when she trailed off and looked away.

"I wanted to ask what *you* thought of it, especially since you weren't at the meeting. I wasn't even aware if you knew what was going on."

Now was the time to tell her why I needed her.

"I need a copy of that merger deal. I need a copy of Southwood's financials, and I need a copy of your findings. I need anything to prove negligence on behalf of my uncle to present to the Board of Directors on Monday."

"Monday?"

"That's when I scheduled the meeting."

"You scheduled it when you were alive."

I shrugged. "Dead or alive, it's still happening."

"Will, this is crazy. You're a well-known figure in this city. How long do you think it will be before the SFPD realize it's not your body in the morgue?"

"I only need the weekend to get in touch with a few trusted people," he said. "They won't be able to confirm Troy's identity with the way he was killed, and I'm banking that even if Sergeant Daniels puts a rush on my dental records, they won't be back until Monday. By then, I'll be ready to come out of hiding."

That look came over her face again, and this time, it didn't go away. I could read it more clearly now, and it was worry.

"What's wrong?"

"I can't do this for you, Will."

"Why? Conscience? The man is a murderer. You said yourself there was something wrong with the deal. All I need is for you to get me the proof."

"I can't. I couldn't even if I wanted to."

"What's that supposed to mean?"

She paused just before she dropped a bombshell on me.

"It means I don't work at Lomax anymore. Jay Lansing fired me this afternoon."

CHAPTER FIVE

Colleen

$\mathcal{J}$ was a nervous wreck.

I'd left Lomax Industries this afternoon with my things packed in a box and stuffed in my trunk, not expecting to ever set foot in this building again. Several hours later, I was back with Will inside my car, tucked in the back seat out of sight and waiting for me to break into Lansing's office and get any information he might have about the merger.

There was a back entrance that wasn't typically guarded that I used to get inside. I knew my pass key had stopped working the moment Jay Lansing had Human Resources issue me my termination papers. However, Will's pass key, surprisingly did still work.

"I'm dead," he said, handing the key card over to me on the drive over here. "There's no threat of me breaking in."

I got inside relatively easy and took the elevator up to the Executive floor. I borrowed Will's baseball cap to cover my hair and kept my head low to avoid the security cameras. Still, by the time I reached Jay Lansing's office, I was seriously having second thoughts about this whole plan.

What if Will was wrong? Yes, undeniably someone came to his home intending to kill, and yet I knew nothing about his friend, Troy. Isn't it possible that Troy may have had enemies who knew he was staying at Will's place for the weekend? What if all this had nothing to do with Will?

I should have followed my first instinct and driven straight toward the police station instead and threatened that if he didn't walk in there and ask to speak to Sergeant Daniels, I would have. But I didn't do that, because Will had done a good job at convincing me that corporate conspiracy was real.

Was Will convincing you or was it his baby blues?

The little voice inside of me couldn't help but whisper that, but I ignored it, refusing to believe that I just might be getting sucked in by his charm—again.

The elevator doors opened to a quiet and dark hallway. I took a moment to mentally prepare myself for what I had to do and then took off for Jay's office. The oak double doors leading to his Executive Suite were locked and only three people had keys: Jay, his assistant and Will. I pulled Will's copies from my pocket and unlocked the door. At the last moment, I turned around to see if anyone spotted me then let myself in, closed the door and took a look around.

The rain had finally stopped. The clouds and fog moved on letting the moon finally have the night back. Its glow shown through the open blinds of the office and the San Francisco city lights and the lit Oakland Bay Bridge were a beautiful sight from the large picture windows.

I went straight to the desk and again, with the help of Will's credentials, I used his security clearance to gain access to Lansing's computer files. Working fast, I searched the computer and quickly found the merger documents with Southwood, along with my team's financial reports and findings and uploaded it all to a flash drive I'd brought with me. As the files were being copied, I kept looking up at the door, certain someone was going to walk in the office at the wrong time and see me committing corporate theft. My heart hammered against my chest and fear had a hold on me that wouldn't let go. I swore I heard noises in the hallway. Where was Jay? Where was his assistant?

I stared at the percentage bar as if it were a lifeline.

40%....45%....50%....

I cursed Will for putting me in this predicament. I cursed myself for having this ridiculous crush on my boss, too weak to tell him no and not being able to forget our night and how much I wanted a second and third night.

60%....65%....

If anyone caught me, I would be arrested. Several minutes passed as the blue progress line crept forward at an achingly slow pace. Just as I was about to lose my nerve and snatch the thumb drive out of the computer, the progress bar sped up and the documents were fully uploaded.

I removed the drive, tucked it in my purse and took a second to make sure I hadn't disturbed anything before dashing for the office door. I opened it slowly, poked my head out and saw no one in the outer office. I stepped out, closed the door softly behind me and then went to the double doors that would lead me out to the hallway.

I took several deep breaths to calm my racing heart, took hold of the door knob and twisted it. It opened soundlessly. I peeked out to find the hallway was still empty and quiet. I moved fast to the bank of elevators and jabbed the 'down' button furiously.

"Come on, hurry up," I said, looking around for anyone who might come from around the corner.

I had no idea what time the emergency meeting was scheduled. But there were a good number of cars in the employee parking lot, so it was safe to say that the building was filled with people who knew me and knew I wasn't supposed to be here.

My blood pressure rose with each number lighting up as the elevator passed every level on its way to the 25th floor. Finally, came the blessed sound of the 'ding' when it arrived. The doors opened, and I flung myself inside and hit the button to close the doors. Just as they began to shut, I heard someone's command.

"Hold that, please."

But I didn't hold the doors. I couldn't even move. Instead, I stood there, frozen as the doors slowly closed and I got only a few second's glimpse of Jay Lansing staring back at me.

CHAPTER SIX

Will

If her hair brushed across my forearm one more time, I was going to lose it.

We made it back to Colleen's house without a problem, but I noticed the moment she got into the car and I sped us away from the Lomax building, something had changed. Her mind seemed to be on other things, and when I asked her if she was okay, she said in a simple tone that my uncle had seen her. She said it as though it were nothing when it was everything.

"He saw you? Where? What happened? He just let you go?" I asked these questions in rapid fire succession, all the while looking in the rearview mirror for any sign of the police chasing after us.

She held up the flash drive. "Let's just get home, so I can show you what I found. I'll explain everything."

When we got back to her place, I made a beeline for her laptop and inserted the flash drive. Together we scanned the documents looking for any proof that I wasn't being para-noid. But as crazy as it sounds, something else was taking hold of my mind more than my uncle's attempted takeover of my company, and that was Colleen's strands of soft brown hair that constantly brushed against my forearm each time she leaned forward to study information on the documents. I had the urge to gently pull that hair and force her to look up at me as a way to get her undivided attention. I wanted to look into those dark brown, silent eyes of hers and see if I affected her as much as she affected me.

"Okay, this is what alarmed me to begin with," Colleen said, jerking me from my thoughts. "Southwood has grown 10% annually. I traced their income growth back as far as seven years, and it's like clockwork."

"What do you think it means," I asked.

She turned from the monitor and looked at me. "I believe some of their revenue is off the books, deliberately hidden to cover up what could be causing their rapid and predictable growth. Like I said before, it may even be illegal."

I sat back in the desk chair eyeing the figures she pointed out to me. "And you told Jay all of this?"

"Of course, I did. It's my job. But he shut me and any further investigation down. He didn't want anything to come up that could delay the merger. But I didn't give up. I kept insisting he halt the merger, but he refused. I can't prove it, but I know that's why I was fired. He cited performance issues."

"Bullshit," I said. I may not have taken my duties as CEO very seriously in the past, but I stayed involved enough to know that Colleen was damn good at her job.

"I can't believe he just let you leave the building. You're sure he didn't say anything to you?"

She shook her head. "He looked shocked when he first saw me, and then…nothing. The elevator doors closed."

"Still, he could've called security, but he didn't."

I let those thoughts go for the moment and concentrated on the documents in front of me.

"You said you thought about bringing all of this to me. Why didn't you?"

"You never came into the office."

"I live next door to you, Colleen. Try again."

She looked away, embarrassed, and I knew immediately what she was thinking.

"You thought I wouldn't care or even be remotely interested."

She looked at me. "I'm sorry. The deal was very profitable, and…"

"Why would I care when that was more money for me, right?"

"I said I'm sorry. I can see now you care more about the company than I thought. I misjudged you."

"Are you saying you believe me?"

"I believe there's something wrong with the merger, but to be honest, I can't get my head around your uncle wanting to kill you to ensure the deal goes through. All he would have to do is get enough board members to vote against you. The merger would proceed with or without your vote."

"Troy is dead."

"And maybe he had his own enemies."

"Troy didn't have any enemies, goddammit," I said, slamming my hand on the desk. "My uncle came after *me*. He wants me gone, but he killed my friend, instead."

She let that go before responding. "Regardless, I still think you should consider talking to the police."

I stood from the desk and glared at her. "You still think I'm making this shit up. That I'm just paranoid."

"No, but I think there may be a plausible explanation. Listen, I agree there's a problem with the numbers, and I agree that this should be brought to the shareholders meeting on Monday. But other than that, I can't get involved, Will."

I wanted to rail at her some more, but I knew she was right. It wasn't her battle to fight this or prove my uncle wanted me out of the way. If I was going to take him down, it was up to me to prove my accusations.

"Fine," I said. "You bring your findings to the shareholders meeting on Monday with me. It'll bear more weight if they hear it from you. I'll prove the rest."

"You want me to go with you? I'm not even supposed to be at Lomax. I was fired, remember?"

"Well, lucky for you, I'm the CEO, and I'm rehiring you."

That seemed to surprise her. "Th-thank you."

"You're welcome."

She left the room, and I took that time to remove the flash drive, tuck it away somewhere safe and shut down her laptop. When she came back, her arms were loaded down with pillows, sheets and blankets.

"The couch is comfortable enough," she said.

I took the linen from her and nodded my silent thanks. "Just give me a couple of days, and then I'll be out of your hair."

She also replied with a nod, and then she muttered a good night and turned to leave. I dropped the sheets onto the couch and then watched the gentle sway of her hips as she walked away, enticing and teasing me.

"Colleen."

She turned with one foot poised on the stairs, her hand grasping the banister.

"Yeah?"

"It's not the first time you misjudged me. You assume a lot about me. The biggest assumption being that I wouldn't have wanted to see you in the morning."

Silence fell like an anchor between us, until she finally spoke.

"As your next-door neighbor, it's obvious you haven't had any problems finding someone to spend the mornings with you."

She turned and continued up the stairs. I opened my mouth to speak, but nothing came out. We both knew that she was right, and there wasn't shit I could say to explain myself.

CHAPTER SEVEN

Colleen

I turned to my side, forcing myself to just go to sleep and not think about him downstairs, lying on my couch.

Why did I have to bring that up? It was clearly on both of our minds, but there had been a silent agreement to just forget about it and definitely never speak about it. But I still saw him. I still saw the woman. I saw him holding her—I saw him looking at me.

Lying in my bed in the dark, I stared up at the ceiling, angry with myself for letting Will see just how much that first night with him, and all the nights that followed without him, still affected me.

It made things easier that he didn't seem to come into the office much, but then I went and made the idiotic move of renting a home right next door to him. Every time I left for work in the morning, or even took out the trash, I was reminded of when we met and how I wasn't honest with him. But nothing reminded me more than when he brought a date home. I wasn't exactly jealous of the women. I was jealous that they would possibly get a second night with him, whereas I never would.

Despite all the adrenaline from tonight, my body must have finally defeated me. I remembered my last thought being about lost opportunities with Will, but I hadn't realized I'd fallen asleep—not until my eyes sprung open to a strong hand clasping my mouth shut.

CHAPTER EIGHT

Will

My body was tired, but I couldn't really fall sleep from having a lot on my mind: Troy's murder, my uncle wanting me dead, the merger and Colleen. But with everything else that was more pressing, my thoughts always circled back to Colleen. I had always been attracted to her. She had a curvy, beautiful body that I'd been fantasizing about exploring again ever since my first night with her. I knew she liked me too, so, what was our problem with each other? Did we only get along when a window separated us?

I felt myself finally beginning to drift off when I heard the slightest sound. So slight, that if there had been anything more than the sound of the ceiling fan whirring above my head, or my own breathing, I wouldn't have heard it. It was coming from her kitchen, where the back patio door was, the same entrance I'd used earlier. Someone else obviously had the same idea—only they weren't knocking.

Quickly and silently, I got up, grabbed the loaded gun from my backpack and crept upstairs to Colleen's room. I didn't want to alert whoever was in the house, so as soon as I entered her bedroom, I moved to her bed and tamped my hand down over her mouth. She immediately struggled against my hold, but I restrained her, and then leaned over her body and whispered directly in her ear.

"There's someone in the house."

I watched as her eyes moved to my face and widen in fear. I said nothing more but put a finger over my lips. When she nodded her understanding to keep quiet, I pulled back the covers and stretched out my hand. She clasped it and allowed me to pull her from the bed.

No words were exchanged as I gestured for her to get inside the walk-in closet, and she did so without question while I used her pillows to create a sleeping form underneath her covers. Then I quickly joined her in the closet, leaving the door cracked only slightly.

Moments later, a shadow moved across the floor, followed by two muffled gunshots. Just as the gunman moved to the bed to inspect it, I came out of the closet in a flash. He whipped around, pointed the gun at my face, but before he could get a shot off, I knocked it from his hand. Fast as lightning, he pulled a knife from his trouser pocket and slashed my left side. I shouted in pain, but managed to dodge his following fatal attacks. I moved away from the closet, and as he stalked me around the bedroom, I noticed Colleen come out, and dash for the bedside lamp. I evaded one more quick slash that dangerously missed my flesh by inches. But it gave Colleen the time she needed to sneak up on our attacker and smash him over the head with the lamp. It stunned him, but he was still on his feet. He turned around, and just that quick, she became his prey. I pulled the gun from my back waist and without a thought, shot him in the back of the head.

Blood and brain matter painted the walls, and Colleen screamed as some of it got on her.

"Are you all right," I asked, stepping over the body and grabbing for her arms because she seemed to be wavering on her feet.

She'd stopped screaming, but shock was written all over her face. "Y-Yes."

"I'm going to check the rest of the house. Clean yourself up and quickly pack a few things. We're getting out of here."

She grabbed for my hand just as I turned to leave. "Be careful."

I nodded and saw what she wasn't saying. That man had come for her. She had just become involved, and it was my fault.

CHAPTER NINE

Colleen

The motel Will found was somewhere further out from the city. It would never make a five-star rating, but the sheets on the two double beds were clean, and the towels didn't smell of mildew. It would be our home for now until Monday morning when Will crashed the shareholder's meeting and accused Jay Lansing of murder and corporate espionage.

Before getting to the motel, we stopped at a drug store, and I bought alcohol and bandages for Will's wounds. As I prepared what I needed, he sat on the edge of one of the beds and took his shirt off. Blood had seeped through his shirt and was now trailing down his side to stain his jeans. He winced from the pain of movement.

"Let me help you," I said, kneeling in front of him and placing cotton bandages against the wound.

"How does it look," he asked, trying to peer down at the cut himself.

"It's not so deep that you need stitches, but I'm going to put alcohol on it and wrap it. This is going to sting."

"It's okay. Just do what you can."

I poured alcohol onto some more cotton bandages and cleaned his wound. He moved only slightly at the stinging sensation, but otherwise remained still, his hard glare fixed on some invisible spot on the opposite wall.

I chanced a glance up at him then back down to focus on stopping the bleeding.

"I didn't know you had a gun. Where did you learn to shoot like that?" I asked.

He shrugged. "My dad was really into guns. He used to take me to the range when I was a kid. I'm not as into them as he was, but I still visit the range every now and then, and I keep a gun for protection."

"You saved my life back there. Thank you."

Another shrug. "I wasn't going to let him hurt you. This is my uncle covering his tracks. It spooked him seeing you at the office. So much so, that instead of calling security, he let you go without a fight and sent his muscle to deal with you instead."

"Do you think he was the same man who went to your house?"

"Probably. If he was, I'm glad the bastard is dead. He killed my friend."

We both went silent for the moment, thinking about a life that was taken unnecessarily. During that time, I finished bandaging his wounds and stood to clean up the mess I'd made. However, before I turned away, Will grabbed ahold of my wrist and I looked down at his hard, smoldering eyes.

"Do you believe me now?"

"I—"

"Is my left side getting sliced open enough for you to finally believe what I'm telling you?"

I tried to move away, but he grasped my wrist tighter. "Tell me you believe me, Colleen."

"Yes," I said. "I believe you."

His grip loosened, but he didn't let go of my wrist. Instead, he looked down at it and ran his thumb up and down my skin, soft like a caress, and I couldn't help but close my eyes.

"I was trying to forget you," he said, still keeping his eyes on my wrist. "I was trying to forget our night together. It wasn't fair to the women I dated after you, but they were never looking for anything long-term. A lot of women I date only want to be seen with a wealthy trust fund baby. Something to post on their social media pages. They don't expect me to call, and if I do, it's because I need a date to some function I'm attending."

"You don't have to explain—"

"I want to." He looked up at me now. "That woman, the one you saw me with, we'd just come from a party. I brought her home, because I was sick of spending my nights thinking about you. I was frustrated, irritated because even though I was trying to forget you, you seemed to have no problem forgetting me."

I snatched my wrist from his grasp and backed away. "What did you expect me to do? I can't be one of your women looking for social media popularity. You're my boss."

"Me being your boss didn't seem to stop you that first night."

I stood and walked around the double bed to put some distance between us. "I know, and I was wrong to mislead you like that. I should've told you who I was the moment you asked my name. We probably would've shared a few drinks, and that would be it."

"No, Colleen, that wouldn't be it," he said. "I would've still asked you to dance, then to my room, and then to breakfast the next morning."

"And then after that?" I held my breath, waiting for his answer.

"I guess we'll never know, will we?"

Unexpected pangs of guilt and more regret washed over me in waves. I couldn't stand there anymore, looking at him and sharing thoughts of what might've been. I turned, grabbed my overnight bag and headed into the single bathroom to get ready for bed.

CHAPTER TEN

Will

We spent the majority of the weekend in the motel tiptoeing around each other, being too polite. It was as if we knew one of us was about to erupt, but neither of us knew who it was going to be. The only reprieve either one of us got was when Colleen put a baseball cap over her head and went out to get some dinner for us. I was actually glad when Sunday evening had finally come. After I ate dinner, I was going to climb into bed and wait for morning when I would crash that shareholder's meeting and begin taking my life back.

Colleen came back with not only Mexican food for dinner, but a suit for me.

"It's not tailored, but it's good enough to make you look like a CEO," she said, handing the garment bag to me. "I hope it fits."

"Thanks," I said. "I'll be sure to put a little extra in your Christmas bonus."

She didn't smile, but looked at the wound on my side. "Sit down. Let me change the bandage."

I sat in an armchair in the corner of the room, while she grabbed her gauze, bandages and alcohol. I watched her, as she walked timidly toward me with supplies in hand.

"Something wrong?"

She shook her head, knelt down in front of me and said nothing as she worked.

"You were right," I said. "The wound isn't too deep. "The bleeding seems to have slowed a lot."

She only nodded, and I decided to say nothing more and just let her finish bandaging me up. I looked up at the ceiling, closed my eyes and ran through the events of the last three days. This was all coming to an end tomorrow. I would get justice for Troy, my uncle would go to jail, and I would take over my company and run it like I should have done years ago, instead of handing the reigns over to a man who despised me. I was beginning to feel overwhelmed and just a hint of anxiety, because for the first time, I was going to be responsible for and lead hundreds of men and women who came to work for my company—my family's company. I'd spent too many years caught up in ridiculous shit, stupid rich boy shit, and now finally, I wanted to do more. Was it Troy's death that caused this change in me? No, seeing his life wasted over mine just solidified it. I had wanted a change for a long time. I wanted to be the man I was supposed to be when I met her.

She was confident, beautiful and accomplished. I knew it instantly that night. And when I found out she worked for me, I couldn't stay away, so I attended the meetings, knowing she'd be there. I sat at the long boardroom table, not knowing a damn thing about what was being discussed, but only wanted to hear her voice, hear that confidence once again that turned me on to the point I was in pain.

Soft hands were moving along my side. I looked down and saw Colleen moving her hand along the fresh bandage. Then her fingers touched my bare skin. She was hesitant, but I kept very still, allowing her to do whatever she needed. She trailed her fingers slowly to the front of my chest, moving from my stomach all the way up to the breastbone. That's when she looked up at me, and the air stilled around us.

Without a word, she gently pushed me back into the armchair and undid the buttons and zipper of my jeans and pulled them off with my briefs. Then she lowered her head over my lap and took me into her mouth. I inhaled sharply, moving my hips to encourage her to take all of me inside her mouth. She moaned and I leaned my head back to stare up at the ceiling, not believing this was actually happening.

It wasn't long before the feeling of her full lips around me was becoming too much for me. I looked back down at her, took her soft hair in my hands, just like I'd always fantasized about and thrust my hips some more. Colleen took all of me, and I could only stand the pleasure for so long. I didn't want it all to end right here. I wanted to be inside of her.

I moved away, taking a moment to catch my breath before I spoke.

"Stand up and take your jeans off," I said.

She smiled and stood over me, undoing her jeans and then slowly and tortuously pulling them over her full mocha hips and thighs until they were at her feet. She kicked them away then pulled her top over her head and unhooked her bra. I sat forward in the chair, took her waist in my hands and kissed and licked her stomach lightly while pulling down her panties. When they, too were at her feet, I forced her thighs apart and sat her down to straddle me.

I was hard and ready for her, and she was soft, wet and ready for me. The moment I entered her, the sounds of moans filled the room as though we'd been sent back to the night we met, remembering the feel of each other. I held her breasts then took my time lightly grazing my tongue over her erect nipples, being led by the sounds of her whimpers and sweet pleas for more.

"Look at me, Will," she breathed. "Look at me like you did when you fucked her. Keep your eyes on me."

I wrapped my arms around her waist, keeping my eyes locked with hers as she began to rock back and forth against me. Goddamn.

Della. That had been her name. I had her in the same position. Her back was to the window, and she was crying out as I moved her in and out of me in rapid succession. I had my eyes closed, thinking of someone else, and when I opened them, there she was. Standing at her own window, her eyes on Della and me. I had forgotten to draw the drapes that evening before I left for the party, and I nearly stopped, embarrassed that Colleen was seeing us. But before I could move Della off of me, Colleen did something that caused my breath to catch.

"Keep looking at me," Colleen said, rocking harder. "Don't stop."

I felt the familiar explosion building up inside of me, but I had to, needed to tamp it down, because I wanted to be inside of her for as long as possible.

"Will, please," she said, grasping me tighter around the neck. "I need to see it. Let me see it!"

I knew what she needed. She wanted to see that intense look of excitement as I neared climax. It was the look I gave her that night while Della rode me. But it was all for Colleen. I wanted her to see just what she did to me. How goddamn good she made me feel whenever I thought of her, whenever I thought of being inside of her.

Colleen's rhythm increased, and I took her hair, wrapped

it around my fist, held on and let her lead me to the edge of the cliff.

"Please," she cried out as her orgasm swept and crashed over her, and that was what I'd been waiting for.

I roared as I emptied myself inside of her, holding her close as our bodies tightened and shuddered. As I slowly came back down, I thought back to that one gesture from her that stopped me from closing the drapes.

A simple head shake.

CHAPTER ELEVEN

Colleen

I woke up a little past six on Monday morning, disappointed to find Will and his belongings already gone. I had expected he would want to be on his own when he entered Lomax Industries, but part of me still wondered if maybe I had this coming, considering I'd done the same thing to him. I lifted my head to look around the room and found a note on the pillow beside me that read:

I thought I'd repay the favor since you can't go home yet. See you at the meeting. Stay safe.

-W

I looked over at the other bed and smiled at the sight of a simple black blazer and pencil skirt with shoes and handbag to match. I didn't know how he planned to get into the meeting later this morning without causing a heap of attention, but I figured a man with his money and resources had ways of getting around things. I rose from the bed and noticed several spatters of blood staining the sheets. Will's wound must have opened up while we were making love. In the middle of our rush to make up for lost time, I'd forgotten about his near miss with the attacker. My heart sped up as I thought about what would've happened if Will hadn't heard the man enter my house that night. Now, I would soon come face to face again with the man who not only fired me, but wanted me and his nephew dead.

I took my time showering, applying makeup and dressing into my new clothes. Then checked out and made my way downtown to the Financial district and Lomax Industries headquarters.

* * *

was surprised to find my credentials worked to get into the building and guessed Will must have pulled strings fast to get me reinstated. Exiting the elevator on the 25th floor, I immediately went to my office and greeted my assistant, who was shocked to find me there. I dismissed her questions and got up to speed on the Board and Shareholder's meeting. A few minutes before nine, I made my way to the conference room. The moment I entered the room, I came to a full stop at the sight of Will sitting in the CEO's chair at the head of the table.

"Good morning, Colleen," he said. His eyes connecting with mine and his smile was brilliant and silently telling me he remembered what happened between us last night. He was wearing the suit I bought for him, and it fit him well, making him look like the CEO and man I wanted like nothing else.

"Please have a seat."

I took a seat a few chairs down from him and among my colleagues and Board members who still had shocked expressions on their faces at seeing Will. When I was settled,

I looked up and for the first time, noticed a familiar face standing off to the side and beside him—Sergeant Lena Daniels. Will must have gone to see her this morning and filled her in on what had happened this weekend. She glanced at me, nodded a silent greeting, and as usual, I couldn't tell what she was thinking.

Howard Jakes, head of Research and Development, stood and cleared his throat. "Will, we heard you were dead. Jay made a statement and everything. We even had a meeting this past weekend about how we were going to proceed, and here you are alive. What happened?"

"Sit down, Howard," Will said in a calm and firm tone. "I told you everything will be explained." He looked around. "It seems we're waiting for just one more person."

As though he'd been summoned, Jay Lansing walked into the boardroom not five seconds after Will spoke. All eyes were on him as he entered, and the moment he set his eyes on Will and then me, I knew it. The horror, shock and guilt melded together so perfectly on his face, and in an instant, I felt sick. He tried to have his nephew killed all in an effort to take over the company. Then he issued a death sentence to me because I threatened his progress.

"Come in, Uncle Jay," Will greeted, still remaining seated in his chair. "Take a seat and let's get this meeting started."

Jay recovered as best he could. "Will, my God! I was told —we all heard you were dead!" He then turned to Sergeant Daniels. "What is this? You told me he'd been killed. What kind of game is your department playing?"

"Sit down!"

I turned at the sound of Will's command and noticed that he looked as though he wanted to commit murder himself. Jay looked from him to Sergeant Daniels then hesitantly sat down at the opposite end of the table. Will glared at him for a moment longer, then turned to his assistant, Selma who was in charge of recording the minutes.

"This meeting of Lomax Industries Board of Directors and Shareholders will come to order."

I admitted I was both surprised and impressed at how Will carried and conducted his duties so far as CEO. From the moment I'd been hired on and subsequently pretended our relationship was nothing more than business, I couldn't remember a time when he took charge of important meetings. He left that responsibility to Jay, and if he even bothered to attend, he would sit off to the side, looking bored and as though he'd rather be anywhere else.

But this was a new Will I was seeing. Maybe becoming a target had caused a change in him. Or maybe he had always been a good businessman and was just never given a chance to show it.

"First order of business it to terminate Jay Lansing and relieve him of his duties as Chief Operating Officer at Lomax Industries effective immediately."

The room erupted, yet Will ignored the chaos, still remaining calm yet determined in his decision.

"Along with Mr. Lansing's termination, I am hereby cancelling the merger with the Southwood Corporation."

"What the hell is this, Will?" Jay stood, his face beet red with fury.

Will gestured to Selma who grabbed a stack of binders and began placing them in front of each person sitting at the table.

"You didn't hear me the first time? You're fired," Will said. "And your merger is cancelled."

"What gives you the right? You're supposed to be dead!"

"But I'm not dead. And neither is Ms. Strayer. Your man screwed that up too."

"What the hell are you talking about," Jay asked, looking

horrified as Selma placed a binder in his hand.

"Everyone, open your binders and turn to the first tab."

Many did as Will ordered, albeit timidly. Others, looked around the room, still unsure of what was going on. When I turned the page and saw the document, I looked up at Will with a grateful smile. It was all here: the analysis of Southwood that Jay had tried to suppress. My investigation results, suspicions and recommendations were all here for the shareholders and board members to see.

"My CFO and her team did their due diligence and the numbers speak for themselves," Will said. "I will give you all a moment to review her findings, but I am cancelling the deal." He then turned to his uncle. "You tried to get in bed with a company that is suspected of having illegal dealings and ignored the advice of your CFO. Instead, you fired her for raising objections. That's the first reason I'm firing you."

"You little bastard. You have no right! You haven't wanted to run this company since it was handed over to you," Jay said, seething. "You gave me the reigns while you concerned yourself with money and fucking everything in a skirt. I've been here since before you were being breastfed. I'm not going anywhere!" He then turned his wrath on me. "I object to this entire meeting on the basis that Colleen Strayer isn't supposed to be here. I fired her last Friday. I'm calling security to have her removed and then I'm adjourning this meeting until you and I have had a chance to speak in private, Will."

"Call them for yourself, because the only person leaving here is you. I rehired Colleen, because she did her job." Will paused and calmly rose to his feet. "And for your information, I have every right as CEO and majority shareholder. A position you tried to relieve me of Friday night, which is the second reason I'm firing you."

"He's insane," Jay said to the room at large. "He comes

back from the dead to cancel a very profitable merger and issues terminations? I demand to put in a vote of no confidence against him."

Will chuckled. "Good luck with that. Everyone turn to tab seven in your binders."

Murmurs continued around the table until everyone was on tab seven. Then a hushed silence fell across the room as we all tried to digest what we were seeing. Even Jay, whose own binder remained shut, leaned over one of the board member's shoulders to see exactly what had everyone's attention. My eyes shot over to him as guilt and rage battled for control over his face. He stood in such a flash that his chair toppled over behind him.

Sergeant Lena Daniels, with a uniformed officer, took her cue and approached him with her handcuffs out and ready.

"Jay Lansing, you're under arrest for conspiracy to commit murder. You have the right to remain silent. Anything you say or do may be used against you in a court of law…"

She continued to recite his rights as she clicked the handcuffs in place. As the uniformed officer led him out of the room, he demanded that his assistant call his lawyer, followed by a string of curses and threats hurled at Will.

When he was gone, I looked back down at the laminated photos inside the binder. There were two columns where on one side was the man who attacked Will and me Friday night, along with his lengthy arrest record, and the other side showed Jay Lansing handing him money.

I glanced up at Will, who still remained steadfast and poised after all of the excitement. While everyone went into an uproar around us, he stared back at me, reading the question in my eyes.

He shrugged. "Money buys a lot of good private investigators."

CHAPTER TWELVE

Colleen

A month after Jay Lansing was arrested on two counts of conspiracy to commit murder, an investigation into the alleged illegal financial activity of the Southwood Corporation was officially opened. The San Francisco business world was having a field day with the news of Lansing's arrest, Southwood's alleged fraudulent activity, and not to mention Will's rise from the dead and his image going from "Trust Fund Playboy" to "CEO of a Global Enterprise".

For a short while, my home was a better rated hotel while Sergeant Daniels conducted her investigation against Jay Lansing, which meant both my and Will's houses were official crime scenes. When she notified me her investigation was concluded, I returned home and as soon as I entered my house, I smelled a trace of cleaning fluid. I dropped my keys and purse on a small table by the door and picked up a handwritten note.

I called in a favor and had your place cleaned for you. It's the least I could do to thank you for letting me come in out of the rain.
-W

Inside my bedroom, I noticed everything was neat and orderly as though nothing had been disturbed. But most startling, was the absence of blood on the walls and a dead body lying on the floor. The cleaning fluid smell was stronger in here, and I guessed Will's people had the carpet shampooed. I silently thanked him, and just like always, thoughts of him came racing back.

As the weeks passed, I stayed on as Chief Financial Officer, thrilled to be able to continue to do what I loved, but conflicted because it meant I couldn't be with Will. For over a month, we've been nothing but professional around each other. It was as though there was once again an unspoken agreement between us to pretend that another passionate night never happened. Or maybe I'd made the agreement with myself. In any case, I'd finally gotten to that point where I couldn't pretend anymore.

CHAPTER THIRTEEN

Will

It was driving me insane. I wanted to be with her, but I wanted her to want me, too. Not because we shared a few days of danger, adrenaline and sex, but because she genuinely wanted to be with the man I was—flaws and all.

It was raining again when I came home that night. I stayed at the office late, still getting accustomed to my new role as active, rather than passive, CEO. I was serious about being an integral part of running my family's company, but that meant I had to take several meetings with Chief staff and their teams to understand the workings of every department. I was also conducting interviews for a new COO, so needless to say, my days were much fuller than they used to be during my idol, playboy days. But I preferred it—anything to keep from thinking about Colleen.

When I pulled into my driveway, I looked over at her house as had been my habit from the first day she moved next door. A feeling of déjà vu came over me when I saw it was dark inside as it had been that rainy Friday evening.

I got out of my car and went inside, pausing at the foyer entrance just like I'd been doing for the past month. The cleaning crew did a good job, but it would never erase the image of Troy lying there on the floor with half of his face missing. I paid for his funeral expenses and sent his family flowers and gifts, but I knew it would never be enough to replace the man himself.

Thinking of Troy made me think that maybe it was time to move. Not only because of his murder, but my feelings for Colleen were growing stronger every day, and I couldn't continue living next door to her if she didn't feel the same way. At first, it gave me a thrill to be able to see her as much as I wanted, but now that we were back to pretending to be strangers after everything we went through…I couldn't do it anymore. I couldn't go back to that.

I took off my jacket, went into the living room and turned on the lamp beside the sofa. My plan was to relax and watch a little TV before going to bed, but then out of the corner of my eye, I saw a light go on. I turn my head to the right. The drapes on my bay windows were drawn shut, but I could still see her silhouette through them. I crossed the room in two quick strides, yanked the curtains open and peered out through the rain.

She must have been home for a while, because I could see she was dressed in jeans that hugged her hips and a t-shirt that clung to her full breasts. I just stood there, waiting for her to give me a sign, a signal, anything. When she opened her mouth only slightly, but said nothing, I accepted it greedily and nodded my head.

Instantly, Colleen backed away from the window, and a second later, the lights went out. I let the curtains drop, and then stepped back to take a few deep breaths. I then turned and headed for the front door, impatient to be near her again. I waited a few seconds and then opened it just in time to see her, her gorgeous brown skin wet from the rain and her hand raised to knock. I said nothing, but grabbed her raised hand, pulled her inside and slammed the door.

CHAPTER FOURTEEN

Colleen

I didn't have the foresight to bring an umbrella or even put on a jacket. I just ran the short distance, showed up at his door, raised my hand to knock and was pulled inside his house. He slammed the door closed, pushed me up against it and kissed me like a starving man. I moved my hands across his broad shoulders and back, aching to get as close to his body as possible and to touch as much of him as I could. My clothes and hair were wet, and my face was cold from the rain, but it felt so good against his body heat. He then broke the kiss to brush my hair away from my face and lift my damp shirt over my head. We both fought to undo the buttons of his dress shirt and trousers, while he sucked the rainwater from the tops of my breasts. I feverishly unhooked my bra, let it fall to the floor and cupped my breasts for him. I watched as he licked and sucked me with greed and grew moist at the thought of him inside of me. He released my hard nipples, and in seconds, I felt his hot mouth on my neck, while one of his hands unzipped the tops of my jeans and delved inside and cupped me. I cried out as he trapped my hands above my head, leaving me immobile while he continued to kiss my neck with his other hand moving inside my panties and making me wet with anticipation. It felt too good to stop, so I lifted one leg above his waist, which only encouraged him to shove his fingers deeper inside of me and move in and out in quick bursts.

"Will, my God!" I screamed, rubbing against him and meeting his fingers with each thrust. I was not opposed at all to come right here in the doorway.

Will chuckled, knowing what I was trying to do. He tormented me even more by removing his hands and fingers and then lifted and carried me to the couch. When my back touched the soft cushions, I shoved my jeans and panties down my hips and only got a glimpse of his full, powerful body before he followed me onto the couch, spread my legs apart and entered me. The instant we felt each other, we moaned in unison, not only from pleasure, but from the relief of finally coming together after so many weeks apart.

"I've wanted you again and again ever since that first night," he said, gripping the arms of the sofa and moving his body in a sensual rhythm that had me clawing his back for more.

"I've wanted you, too. Don't talk, please!" I was already crazy with desire for him, but I could feel the orgasm rising inside of me with each word he spoke.

"Just like this. It was never enough," he said, his breathing increasing, his stroke intensifying.

"Will!"

From the three days we shared together, followed by weeks of fantasizing about him, to the mindless pleasure in his doorway. The pressure inside of me had been building for too long, and I was on the edge, ready to explode. I needed him, all of him.

"Once with you was never enough."

My orgasm came violently, causing me to shake and shudder while crying out Will's name in long, guttural moans. I trapped his waist between my legs and arched my back for every last drop of that exquisite feeling of release. As I soared, I smiled at the sounds of his own roars of pleasure chasing after mine.

* * *

"Don't quit."

I was on top of Will as we lay sprawled together on his couch, staring at the fire he'd made. I raised my head and brushed my damp hair away from my face to look at him.

"How did you know?"

"For the past couple of weeks, I know you've been thinking about it. I may have rehired you, but something's changed. You seem different. Unhappy."

I shook my head. "It's not me who's changed, Will. It's you. That night we met, you had a look in your eyes when you talked about the company. You said they didn't need you, and at first, I thought you looked sad, but that wasn't it. Now I know that look was impatience. You've been waiting for the chance to prove yourself, and here it is. You're just what the company needs to move forward."

"Thanks, but what does that have to do with you wanting to leave?"

I didn't immediately answer, but sat up and grabbed for his shirt to put around me. He continued to lay back on the couch, studying me with one arm resting underneath his head.

"What is it," he asked.

I let go a long and deep exhale. "It was easier for me when you were just a playboy. I know that sounds terrible, but it's true. Life was easier for me when you didn't have much interest in the company."

"And now?"

"Now that I see this new side of you, I like you, even more than I did when we first met."

"Which means we can't work together," he finished, sitting up. His eyes flashed angrily in the firelight. "Do you always have to make the fucking decisions when it comes to us?"

"Will, it would be unprofessional—"

"To hell with that!" He got up, shoved on his trousers, and paced around the living room. After a few minutes, he stopped and turned to me with his entire body brimming with frustration.

"I grew used to having one-night stands, and I tried to fit you in that box, too. But you're not a one-night stand. I knew it from the first moment I met you, and it scared the hell out of me. When I woke up and found you gone that morning with no way to contact you, I was pissed. I couldn't stop thinking about you. I still can't stop thinking about you. Then I walk into a mandatory meeting one day, and there you were. But you weren't the same. I was a stranger to you."

His words were making me nervous. I could feel my resolve, the rules I'd set for myself beginning to break down. He was being so open with me, and I suddenly wanted to do the same for him.

"That woman you brought home that night wasn't your CFO. She was a woman you met one night at a party. I wanted to be her so badly, because she could be with you, and I couldn't."

I paused. "That's why I shook my head while you were with her. I didn't want you to stop. I was pretending to be her and pretending to be with you. I wanted to see and feel what it would have been like if I didn't work for you—if I was just another girl you met at a party."

Silence reigned and for a long time, he stood over me, his face unreadable. Then he kneeled in front of me, and I saw that his eyes had returned to their soft blue glow, but there was still heat in his gaze.

"We can find a way to work together and be together, too. All I'm asking is for a chance to try. Just stay with me, Colleen. I don't want to lose you to another company." He paused. "I don't want to lose you to anyone."

I pushed away all logic and reason and pulled him back onto the couch with me for a deep and satisfying kiss. His hands slowly roamed over my breasts, circled my erect nipples then traveled down to my waist and stomach to rest between my legs. Before I began to pant and plead for him to take me again, I pulled back and braced my hands over his chest.

"Where are we going for our second date?"

He smiled in that sexy way I found so irresistible, and then continued to let his hands explore between my thighs. When his fingers reached that most sensitive part of me, I arched my back into him and closed my eyes. The next sound I heard was Will whispering into my ear.

"Stay the night, and the second date will be in the kitchen for breakfast."

* * *

Thank you for reading EXPLICIT! If you enjoyed this novella, you'll love the next book in the EX FILES series, EX FACTOR.

Parker is being targeted by some very dangerous people, and the only one who can keep her alive is the man she told herself she didn't love anymore.

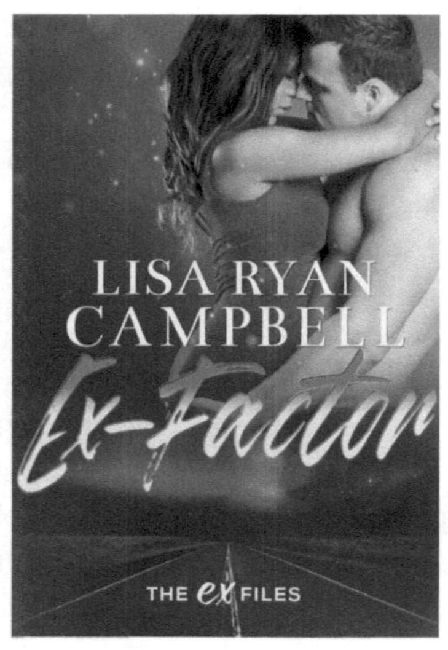

ONE-CLICK EX FACTOR NOW >
"A perfect, sexy afternoon read."
"True romantic suspense."

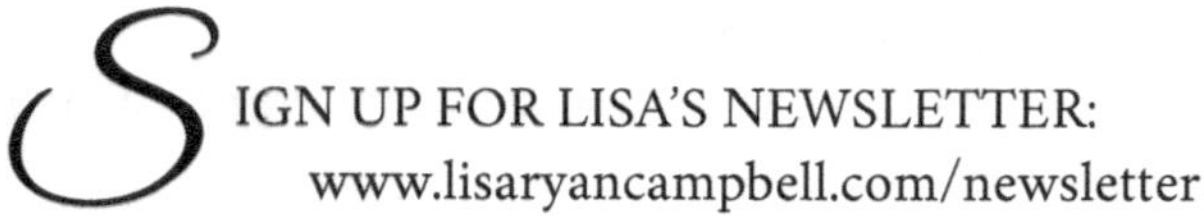

SIGN UP FOR LISA'S NEWSLETTER:
www.lisaryancampbell.com/newsletter

. . .

And for more steamy romantic suspense, check out EXILED.

Gray wants Shannon back in his arms again. But how can he trust her when she confessed to his brother's murder?

ONE-CLICK EXILED NOW >

"Prepare to be wowed."

"This is romantic suspense at its finest."

Award-winning Author, Lisa Ryan Campbell began writing as a small child using her mother's pink typewriting paper. Years later, she decided it was important to get a "real job" and attended Arizona State University to major in English with the goal of continuing on for both a Master's and Doctorate degrees in English and teach at the college level.

In 2002, Lisa graduated with a Bachelor's degree in English Literature and an Ancient Egyptian romance novel she wrote in her spare time. She decided then she would not be continuing on to graduate school, but instead joined Romance Writers of America and focused on her true love.

Lisa is an avid traveler and has seen many of the world's treasures in Egypt, Peru, Spain, France, Morocco, England, Mexico and the Caribbean. She spends her time mostly at her home in Colorado writing, reading and watching 1940's noir movies. She also loves to laugh, so you may frequently catch her watching reruns of Archer, Veep and The Office.

Sign up for Lisa's newsletter and find out more about her books at www.Lisaryancampbell.com and connect with her on social media.

9 781958 078013